To Noriko and Kenichi

First Chronicle Books LLC paperback edition, published in 2015.
First published in hardcover in the United States of America in 2006 by Chronicle Books LLC.
Originally published in Japan in 2003 by Hakusensha.

ISBN 978-1-4521-4567-9

The Library of Congress has cataloged the previous edition as follows:
    Sakai, Komako, 1966-
      [Ronpåa-chan to fåusen. English]
      Emily's balloon / by Komako Sakai.
        p. cm.
      Summary: A little girl's new friend is round, lighter than air,
      and looks like the moon at night.
      ISBN-13: 978-0-8118-5219-7
      ISBN-10: 0-8118-5219-9
      [1. Balloons—Fiction. 2. Friendship—Fiction.] I. Title.
      PZ7.S143943Em 2006
      [E]—dc22
              2005011283

Manufactured in China.

MIX
Paper from
responsible sources
FSC™ C016973
FSC
www.fsc.org

English text design by Anne Ngan Nguyen.
Typeset in Wendy and Today Sans.

10 9 8 7 6 5 4 3 2 1

Chronicle Books LLC
680 Second Street
San Francisco, California 94107

Chronicle Books—we see things differently. Become part of our community at
www.chroniclekids.com.

One day, Emily gets a balloon.
By the end of the afternoon, the
balloon is no longer just a plaything.
Emily and the balloon are friends. But
~~~~~~~~~~~~~~~~~~~~~~~~~~ ...at
will Emily do?

This beautifully evocative text and illustrations and the timeless innocence of
the story make this deceptively simple
book a classic—at once sweet and
compelling, and filled with the wonder
and discovery of friendship.

Praise for Emily's Balloon:

★ "Perfectly reflects a very young child's worldview. . . . The illustrations
are remarkably expressive." —*The Horn Book,* starred review

★ "A dog-eared favorite in the making." —*Publishers Weekly,* starred review

"A tale of a common childhood experience, tenderly and sweetly told."
—*School Library Journal*

"Sakai's gracefully executed tale illuminates the pure joy with which toddlers
embrace even the most ordinary occurrences. " —*Kirkus Reviews*

A New York Public Library Title for Reading and Sharing
An ALA Notable Children's Book
A Kirkus Reviews Best Children's Book of the Year
A Book Links Best New Book for the Classroom
A Horn Book Fanfare selection
A Child ~~~~~~~~~~~~ the Year

emily's
balloon

emily's balloon

by Komako Sakai

chronicle books · san francisco

One afternoon, Emily got a balloon.

Oops!

The balloon was tied to her finger.

And then it came home with her.

Let's take that off.

Whee!

Uh-oh.

Here you go.

Again?

Emily's mother tied the string in a loop.

And put the loop around Emily's spoon.

Look!

It floats, but it doesn't fly away!

Emily and the balloon went into the yard.

They picked flowers.

Emily made a beautiful crown for the balloon,
and one for herself.

They played house.

Then *whoosh* went the wind.

The balloon! Emily's balloon!

There! In the tree!

It's stuck, Emily. I can't get it down.
I'm sorry.

Emily missed the balloon.
Dinner didn't taste good without it.

We wanted to eat together.

Then we would put on our pajamas,
and brush our teeth,

and go to sleep.

Tomorrow, I'll borrow a ladder and get it down.
  Really?
Really.
  Really and truly?
Really and truly. Goodnight, honey.

But Emily couldn't stop thinking about the balloon.
Was it still there?

She looked.
There it was, nestled in the tree.
It looked just like the moon.

Goodnight.

Komako Sakai was born in 1966 in Hyogo, Japan, and studied art in Tokyo. She worked in textile design before beginning to illustrate children's books. She is the winner of the Japanese Picture Book Prize.